SNAP
SHOT

Robert
SWINDELLS

For Vincent Parmenter, whose quick thinking
gave me the idea for this book

First published in 2005 in Great Britain by
Barrington Stoke Ltd
18 Walker Street, Edinburgh, EH3 7LP

www.barringtonstoke.co.uk

This edition first published 2014

ISBN: 978-1-78112-345-4

Printed in China by Leo

Contents

Chapter 1
Happy Deathday

It was my birthday really, but it *could* have been my deathday. It very nearly was, in fact. My name's Alfie, by the way. Alfie Gott. I live in Straw House. Not *a* straw house like the three little pigs – Straw House is a block of flats. We're on the third floor. Mum, Dad and me. I've got no brothers or sisters.

People think you're spoilt if you're an only child, but I'm not. No way. I have to do chores to get money, and I don't get that much even then. I'd been saving up all year to get this amazing new SLR camera. It had been like trying to push a peanut up Mount Everest with my nose. All that came to an end on my birthday. I've got this uncle, Uncle Harry, and he gave me the SLR for a present! I was so pleased. It was really state-of-the-art and the memory card could store millions of photos. I couldn't wait to get outside and take a few shots.

My mate Lee reckons I'm sad because I like taking pictures, but I don't care. I say to him, "Better than smoking like you, or robbing, like your Scott."

Lee smokes where his mum can't see him, and his big brother Scott shoplifts and picks pockets and stuff like that. He's been inside twice. They're both idiots. Lee thumped me when I said that, but it's true. Taking pictures doesn't give you cancer, and they won't bang you up for it.

But taking pictures *can* be dangerous. It was for me that day ...

"Where are you off to?" Mum said. I was by the door, putting on my hoody. I pointed to the camera that was hung on a strap round my neck. "Just off to take a few photos, Mum."

"What'll you take photos *of?*" she said. "There's nothing but streets out there."

"Streets are good, Mum," I told her. "Lots of people take pictures of streets."

"Yes, and lots of people are daft," she said. "Don't go too far, it'll be dark soon."

You see, it was after school. I'd only just opened my cards and presents. Why do you have to go to school on your birthday? It's not right, if you ask me.

So off I went along the walkway and down the stairs. There's a lift, but it stinks and anyway it's faster to go downstairs on foot. It was getting dark and it was drizzling. The street shone with light from shop windows and cars. There was loads of traffic. When I took a photo, I got white light from headlamps one side and red light from tails and brakes the other. Plus amber flashes here and there. It made a nice shot, and I think I got it just right.

Anyway, there I was on the edge of the pavement, snapping away, and this car drew up and stopped outside a jeweller's. Two guys got out, the one driving the car stayed inside. I only started to watch them because it looked as if one of the guys was hiding something under his coat. But I was busy. I didn't think too much of it. Then the shop window shattered. I looked then all right.

It was an axe the guy had inside his coat. He swung it at the jeweller's window three or four times. Glass flew. It sparkled on the pavement around his shoes. Somebody screamed. The shop door opened and two people came out. They were shouting and waving their arms in the air. The guy with the axe stepped towards them. He lifted the blade in front of their faces. They stopped dead in their tracks like scared characters in a cartoon. The second guy was reaching into the window now. He was scooping up trays of rings and watches.

I was so shocked I didn't even think about my camera. Seconds passed by before I realised I had it in my hand, and I thought about taking a photo.

By this time, one of the men had his arms full of all the trays of jewellery. He was dumping them in the boot of his car. The other man was walking backwards, snarling at the shop assistants and waving his axe …

I got four photos. The two guys as they scrambled back into the car. The driver as he yelled at them to hurry up. The car as it began to move off, with the axeman's head and arm still outside. The last one was of the car coming straight at me.

And that's why I said happy deathday before. The driver had spotted me and my camera. Smile please – only he wasn't smiling. He was bent low over the steering wheel, hunched up like some sort of pyscho. The car came up onto the kerb towards me. I stood frozen till it was nearly too late. At the very last second, as the car's front wheels bounced up onto the kerb, I ducked behind a postbox. The side of the car crumpled as it hit it. The wing-mirror flew spinning past my head. The driver clashed his gears, backed off and the car roared away. I sat on the pavement and was shaking so much I had to cling onto the postbox. A woman tapped me on the back. "Are you all right, dear?" she asked.

Chapter 2
Did You Get His Number?

"Y– yeah, I'm fine," I said as I sat, crouched behind the postbox. I didn't feel all that fine. But people were staring at me. I hate it when everyone looks at you. All I wanted was to get away from there. The woman who had tapped me on the back shook her head. "You're white as a sheet dear. I expect it's the shock. Did you get the car's number?" she asked.

"Huh? What? No, I didn't think of it." I was still shaking.

A guy stepped forward. "*I* did." He waved his phone. You could tell he thought he was smarter than anyone there.

The woman rolled her eyes. "Brilliant," she said. "Have you rung 999?"

"Yeah," the guy said. "The police are on their way."

The woman turned round and said to everyone who was watching, "We'd better all wait. The police'll want statements."

I wasn't going to wait. As soon as she'd turned her back, I slipped away. There's an alley that runs between two shops just there. It leads through to the next street. Somebody yelled "Oi!" as I headed for the dark, but I was off like a rat up a drainpipe. They'd no chance of catching me. I was born here. I know this bit of town like the back of my hand.

Don't get me wrong. I'm not an enemy of the police. That's not why I ran. I knew there was vital evidence inside my camera. Photos that would be very useful to the police. I knew I should hand them over. But there was a problem. *Two* problems really. One, I didn't want to give them the memory card. That meant I had to download the photos onto a computer. And two, I knew who one of the guys was – the guy who liked to do his shopping through broken windows. You won't need three guesses at his name. It was Scott Watford, my mate Lee's brother. Remember him?

Poor old Scott. Yes, I *know* he's a criminal, but he's such a sad one. Two cans short of a six pack, my dad says. People take advantage. They run off and leave him to take the blame. Like I said, he's already been inside twice. I didn't want to be the one to put him away again. I mean, his brother's my best *mate*.

Anyway, that's why I ran off instead of sticking around to do my duty as an honest citizen. But it wasn't long before I wished I'd stayed.

I came out the far end of the alley, turned right and walked away, cool as could be. Nobody had chased me, I knew they wouldn't. I walked along a bit, took another right and then another. I was back on my own street, about 200 metres down from the postbox near where it had all started. It had stopped drizzling. I could see blue flashing lights outside the jeweller's.

I was well and truly over the shakes. In fact I was feeling so calm I decided I'd stroll back to the jeweller's, but on the other side of the road, to see what was going on. I stopped for a second to put up my hood so no one would see it was me. That's when I realised I was being followed.

He was wearing a dark baseball cap and a puffa jacket. He was about 20 metres behind me. He stopped when I stopped. When I start walking again, I realised he started walking. I stopped beyond William Hill's betting shop. I passed it every day and so I know its window is blanked out and there's nothing to see. Yet the guy stopped there, and just stood and looked into the glass as if some drop-dead gorgeous girl was taking a bath in there. That was a real giveaway. I moved on and glanced behind me. He was still following.

I wasn't worried. In fact I was quite excited. It's not every day you fall into a real-life adventure and like I said, I know this bit of town like the back of my hand. I could shake him off anytime I chose. I'd let him shadow me for a bit, then I'd lose him.

I knew what he was after, and why he wanted it. He was after my camera, and he wanted it because he was one of the jewel thieves. Was he the driver? Or the one with the axe? I couldn't remember their faces – apart from Scott's of course – but I might have got a good photo of them. The guy behind me didn't fancy a stretch inside, so he thought he'd get the evidence. After all, how hard can it be to take a camera off a kid?

'Harder than you think,' I said to myself.

The first plan I had was to make him follow me into one of the blocks on our estate. They're like rabbit warrens if you don't know them. Everybody gets lost. Then I thought, 'No, he'll count on catching me by myself so he can scare me or wrestle the camera off me. All I have to do is stay on the streets. He won't dare tackle me in front of hundreds of people.'

So that's what I did. I walked the streets at random. I didn't use alleys of course, or cross any waste ground. I kept stopping to look in windows. That kept him on his toes. It must have driven him mad.

I suppose I knew deep down I was playing a dangerous game. I didn't know then *how* dangerous. If I'd known who I was messing with

I'd have given him the camera *and* asked if he'd like my left arm to go with it.

Chapter 3
Only Had it Half an Hour

I began to work out that the guy who was following me wasn't just any old hit and run criminal when I found I couldn't shake him off. That was the first clue that he wasn't just one of Scott's dodgy mates. I tried every trick in the book and he still stuck to me like glue.

It was six o'clock. The game wasn't funny any more. I knew it'd be a bad mistake to let him see where I lived, whoever he was. On the other hand, Mum'd go crazy if I stayed out any longer. The only thing left for me to do was to go with my original idea – head back to Straw House and hope the maze of stairs and walkways would fool him.

As I pushed open the swing doors at the bottom of the stairs to my block, I looked back quickly. The guy following me was about 50 metres behind me. He was walking fast and he had his hands in his pockets. He'd stopped pretending he wasn't interested – he was looking straight at me. I slipped inside and let the doors bang behind me.

I thought about taking the lift, but everything it does is really, *really* slow. You punch the DOOR CLOSE button and the lift thinks about it for ages. Then it obeys like it's on sleeping pills.

What I did was this – I leaned in and pressed 7. That's the top floor. Then I set off up the stairs. With a bit of luck, the guy following me would get to the lift just as the doors closed. The lights above the lift doors would show him the lift was headed for the top floor. He'd think I was in the lift. He might wait for the lift to come back down or he might go up the stairs. But even if he went up the stairs he probably wouldn't find me. My plan was to hide on the second floor landing, in the little room where the rubbish chute is.

My plan might not work. If the guy checked out all the doors, I'd be stuffed. There was no way out of the room, except down the chute itself. I was sure he was after my camera – probably the photos I'd taken with it. But I'd made up my mind now. He was never going to get my photos, whatever happened. Halfway up the first lot of stairs, I stopped for a second and popped the memory card out of the camera. I slipped it down the inside of my trainer. If the guy caught me, I'd hand over the camera without the card. I hoped he wouldn't check it.

As I carried on up the stairs, I heard the lift come rumbling by. I can't see through concrete, so I didn't know whether the guy was in it or not. I hoped he was. If not, he wasn't far behind me.

I didn't make it as far as the second floor. There was no bulb in the light on the first floor landing, but there, in the gloom, I could see Smithy, Mike and Andy.

"Hello, Alfie," Smithy said. "We were wondering what'd happened to you, weren't we?"

Andy nodded. "Haven't seen you for ages, Alfie. What's that you've got anyway?"

"Just a camera." I hoped he wouldn't be interested in a camera.

Smithy grinned. *"Just* a camera, Alfie? *Just?"* He held out a hand. "Lemme look." I knew I had no choice, so I handed it over.

Smithy whistled. "This isn't *just* a camera. I've seen these online, 500 quid each. And you say it's just a camera. You just don't know about cutting edge technology, that's your trouble." He smirked. "Deserves an owner who appreciates it. What d'you say?"

He turned to his mates and they nodded. "That's it," Mike said. "Wasted on you, Alfie."

"Wasted," Andy said, like he was Mike's echo.

"Tell you what," Smithy said. "We'll take this fine camera off you, and as you've been so good to us, we'll let you keep your ears. How about that?"

"Not good," I say. I know it won't work but I try to talk them out of it anyway. "This camera's a birthday present. From my uncle. I've only had it half an hour."

Smithy smiled. "Didn't know it was your *birthday*, Alfie," he said. He turned to the others.

Hear that, it's Alfie's birthday. I think that calls for a song, don't you?"

Both his friends nodded. They began to sing out of tune,

"Happy birthday to you
  Happy birthday to you
  Happy birthday, dear Alfie
  Happy birthday to you."

As their voices echoed up the stairwell, Smithy jerked his head. "Go on, off you go, or I'll bang your head on the step – one bang for each year of your life."

I wish I'd been brave enough to smash my fist into his face, one smash for each year of his life. Instead it took me all my efforts not to cry.

I turned away and went on up the stairs. Would I bump into the guy that had been following me? I didn't really care any more.

What I didn't know then was that Smithy and I would never meet again.

Chapter 4
Just Like That

I'd got to the second floor landing when there was a loud bang. All noises echo round in these blocks. You get used to ignoring them. But this bang really was loud. Then I heard Mike shout, "No, no, no."

I didn't give a stuff about Mike and his mates. I'd most likely have ignored the noise as usual, and dodged into the second floor rubbish chute room to hide before the guy showed up. But then my brain started to put things together. The guy. The camera. A loud bang. I ran out to the walkway and looked down. A guy had just left the flats and was hurrying away. A guy in a puffa jacket and a baseball cap – and a large camera in his hand.

I went back to the stairs and ran down. I could hear Mike moaning. When I got to the first floor I saw Smithy sprawled face down on the floor. The other two were staring at him. They didn't look as hard as when I'd last seen them. Mike's cheeks shone with tears and Andy's mouth was open, like something you see down the fish market. He heard me and looked up.

"He shot him, Alfie. He came up the stairs and shot him, just like that. Took the camera." He sniffled. "I think he's dead."

I looked down at Smithy. I'd never seen anyone dead before. There was a wet stain on his back, the size of a DVD. It was just below his left shoulder blade.

I nodded. "I think he's dead, too, Andy," I said. "Have you called the police?"

Maybe I sounded really cool, but I wasn't. I really wasn't. I was thinking how I'd played games with the guy who'd done this. I'd led him all over the place. For fun. And all the time he'd had a gun in his pocket. He'd have used the gun on me if he'd got me by myself. Instead of Smithy, it could be *me* going cold on the concrete.

Andy was shaking his head. "No, 'course I haven't called the police. We don't want anything to do with them, Mike and me. In fact we'd better be going." He looked at Mike. "Come on, mate, nothing we can do here."

"Hang on." I looked hard at him. "You can't just walk away, not from this. It's murder. You saw it happen. You're eyewitnesses. The police'll have questions ..."

"I know," Mike said. "That's the whole point. We start answering questions and before you know it, they've got all sorts on us. They might say *we've* done this – killed our own mate." He breaks off and looks at me. "What's so great about that camera? Why did that guy *kill* for it?"

I shrugged. "Dunno. I saw a raid, at a jeweller's. I took some photos. Maybe it was that ... Anyway, it's no good you doing a runner. The police'll know you're always with Smithy. They'll pick you up, then it really *would* look as if you'd done it." I pulled my phone out of my pocket. I'm calling them now, OK?"

"Suppose," Mike mumbled. I pressed nine three times.

I didn't ring the police for Smithy, or for justice, or because it was my duty. I did it because I could feel that memory card in my shoe. The guy with the gun'd soon find the card wasn't in the camera and he'd know who'd got it. He'd be back and I wanted a whole swarm of policemen between him and me when he was.

The policeman who picked up my call thought I was winding him up at first. It took me over a minute to convince him to come. He moved pretty fast once I had, though.

It was the same when I rang Mum, two seconds after I'd talked to him.

"Where *are* you?" she said. "It's after seven, your tea's ruined."

"I'm downstairs, Mum, with a body." Good line that, if you ever get a chance to use it.

She's like, "*Body*? What are you *talking* about? What games are you playing? Get yourself up here, quickly, or I'll send your dad down to get you."

I suppose it's a rotten thing to say, what with Smithy lying there dead and all that, but the next hour was really exciting.

Chapter 5
Moved Him, Have You?

Nee-naw, nee-naw, nee-naw.

I *loved* doing that noise when I was a kid – a police siren. We stood and listened as the police cars came closer. This time the sound was for real. No one was playing at cops and robbers now.

We get loads of police sirens on the estate. You hear them a lot, but you don't often find out who called them, or why. We knew this time. It felt weird, to me, anyway. Mike and Andy have both been in the back seats of police cars a few times. It was different for them.

Next thing, we heard the clatter of boots on concrete. I relaxed a bit – the guy wasn't going to show up now, not with the police about. We watched the stairs. Two police ran up to us. They were puffing and panting. They took a quick look at Smithy. Then one came over to us.

"Which one of you's Alfie Gott?"

"That's me," I said.

"You're the one who called us?

"Yes."

The policeman looked at Mike and Andy. "And what about you two? Why are you here?"

Andy nodded towards Smithy's body. "We're his mates. We saw the bloke shoot him."

"Moved him, have you?"

"N– no."

"Touched anything?"

"No."

"Well don't. This is a crime scene. I'll get your details while we're waiting."

'What are we waiting for?' I asked myself. The second policeman had bent down beside Smithy. He looked at his mate and shook his head. I knew what that meant – I'd seen it on telly. It meant Smithy was dead. I could've told them that, but I guess it was official now. Smithy wasn't Smithy anymore, he was 'the body'.

While the first policeman was getting our names and addresses, the other one talked into his radio. He was doing that when we heard footsteps coming down and Mum turned up.

The first policeman went over to her and stopped her on the bottom step. "You can't come any further madam, this is a crime scene."

Mum looked furious. "I don't *want* to come any further," she said. "I want *him* home, his tea's cold." She stabbed a finger at me.

"We'll have finished with him in a moment," said the officer. "For now, I mean. It's nothing to worry about," he said.

I don't think Mum really registered what had happened. She said she'd expect me home soon, and left without protesting any further.

Mum had just gone back up when two more policemen arrived. They had a reel of that yellow tape they cordon off crime scenes with. It had POLICE LINE DO NOT CROSS printed all over it. The police hung the tape across where Mum had been standing. Then they stuck some across the top of the first flight of stairs. The landing was now cordoned off.

We hadn't got to the important bit yet. The memory card was still in my shoe. I was waiting for the right moment to tell them about it. To be honest, I didn't know when the right moment would be, but it didn't feel like now. Then a policeman in plain clothes showed up and I knew. I'd been waiting for a proper detective. His name was Detective Sergeant Pitt.

"Excuse me," I said, "can I have a word?"

His eyebrows went up as he muttered, "What is it, son?"

"I think I know why Smithy was shot, sir."

He made a face at me. "Do you now? And why was he shot?"

"For this. I took it out of my camera." I stuck two fingers down into my trainer and tweezered the memory card out.

The detective looked at it closely. He frowned. "The gunman wanted this, you think? Why was it in your shoe and not in the camera?"

"He was following *me*, sir, before he got to Smithy. I took the card out of the camera and hid it in my trainer in case he caught me. I didn't know he had a gun."

Then, of course, I had to tell the detective the whole story. I told him about the photos I'd taken of the jewellery shop robbery and all the rest of it. The detective tut-tutted and shook his head when I got to the bit about how I tried all sorts of dodges on the gunman. But, like I said, *I* didn't know he was a gunman, did I?

I was lucky. He let me go home when I'd finished my story. Mike and Andy were taken to the police station for more questioning. I'd had to explain how Smithy came to have my camera, so maybe that's why the police held onto Mike and Andy.

I was in big trouble when I got in. They'd had macaroni cheese for tea. Mine was like the bottom of a plastic flip-flop now. Mum showed it to me, then chucked it in the bin. I had to make myself some beans on toast. Much nicer than macaroni cheese any day if you ask me, but I wasn't stupid enough to say so.

Dad said, "Your Uncle Harry should've had more sense than to give a kid your age a camera worth that much money. And as for you – why'd you take photos of a robbery? Didn't you stop to think it might be a silly thing to do? D'you think robbers would let some kid put them away for years on end?" He snorted. "What if they find out where you live, eh? What if they come here, with their guns and their axes? What if they have a go at your mum? You won't feel so clever then, I'll bet."

I hadn't thought of that. Detective Pitt had kept the memory card, but the gunman didn't know that. What if he *did* come? He'd killed poor Smithy just like that, as if shooting someone was the same as stamping on a beetle.

We watched telly all evening, but I didn't enjoy it. I couldn't relax. I was listening to every little noise, and ours is a very noisy block.

It was even worse in bed. I kept my bedside light on and I put my phone under the pillow. Still, it was well after midnight before I dropped off.

Chapter 6

Two in One Day

"Alfie. *Alfie*." I woke up. Dad was shaking me. It was still dark outside.

"Whassup?" I mumbled. "What time is it, Dad?"

"It's early, son. Listen. I want you to tell this man what you did with the card from that camera."

"*Man?*" I woke up then all right. There was a man behind Dad. He looked enormous in my small bedroom and was wearing a puffa jacket and a dark baseball cap.

Mum was there too. She looked very scared.

I sat up without taking my eyes off the guy. He gave Dad a push. Then he stood over me. "Where is the card?"

"Don't hurt him, please," said Mum. "He's only a child."

"Shut up." He was staring in my eyes. "Where is it?"

"Uh ... I gave it to the policeman." God, was I scared. I wished I had the card so I could let him have it. Then he'd get out of our flat. Dad was right. I'd been really stupid and I didn't feel clever at all now.

"Ah!" He nodded and slid a gun out of his pocket.

"I *told* you," said Dad. "He's a kid, he was scared, they took it off him."

"Shut your stupid mouth," the man snapped.

He turned to Dad and Mum. "Face down on the floor, now."

"What you gonna do?" Dad's voice was a croak. "You can't ..."

"Can't I?" The man turned back to me. "You also, face down, quick," he said.

It wasn't real. I felt like I was in a nightmare. Everything went into slow motion except my brain. Getting out of bed I saw the clock on my bedside table. It was half past three. I thought, '12 hours from now I'll just be coming out of school.' But I knew I wouldn't be. There'd be no more school for me. My mate Lee would see it all over the news – what happened to the Gotts. It'd be like something on the telly. Neighbours would be shaking their heads, saying we were quiet people, kept ourselves to ourselves.

"Let the boy go," said Dad into the carpet. "And my wife. What good will it do to ...?"

"I told you, shut up," the man hissed back at him.

I got down on all fours beside Mum. Then, as I lay down, she lifted her arm and put it over my back. I turned my head sideways so I could look at her. So she'd be the last thing I saw. She was crying, without making a sound. The carpet smelled dusty.

There was a sharp click. That must be the guy doing something with the gun. I thought, 'It'll be now'.

Everything exploded in light and noise.

I thought that was it. That was what it was like being shot. But it wasn't. It wasn't, because the noise and the light didn't stop. Didn't go black or silent.

Now there were voices shouting. Heavy footsteps thumped on the carpet and made my head judder. There were shots – four I think. Then somebody cried out and something fell over with a crash. Mum's arm lifted off me and as I opened my eyes, I saw the room was full of men.

Somebody picked me up. I was on the bed and I was looking at something on the floor. I'd never seen a dead body in my life – now I'd seen two in one day. The gunman lay with his jacket half off, and my bedside table across his legs. He looked surprised, which I suppose he was. I was a bit surprised myself.

There was total confusion at first. People coming and going. Snatches of talk I didn't understand. I remember having a three-way hug with Mum and Dad, which was a first. And a mug of cocoa, which wasn't. Uncle Harry was there for some reason, even though it was the middle of the night. Maybe Dad got him over to give him hell about the camera. If so it didn't work, because he told me not to worry, he'd get me another one.

After what seemed a long, long time, everybody went away and Mum, Dad and I were on our own at last. It was nearly five in the morning and I was shattered. All I wanted was sleep. My room was cordoned off though, like the first floor landing. Crime scene. The guys in white'd be back in the morning to poke through everything.

I slept in my parents' bed. It was like being two years old again. Dad stayed up. He said he might as well get a good start on the day. Said he couldn't sleep anyway.

I didn't have any trouble.

Chapter 7
Coco Pops in Bed

Next day was Friday. It was a school day, but I thought I could get a day off. Well, I'd not had my ration of sleep, had I? Plus I'd been through a hard time. When Mum came to get me up I was ready with my plan. She called from the doorway. I didn't stir. She came in, called louder. I lay still. She bent down to give me a nudge. The second her hand touched me I jumped up suddenly and shouted out, "Yeeeaaaaagh!"

"Sorry," she gasped. "Sorry Alfie, it's only me. Time to get up."

I shook my head and let out a long, dramatic sigh. "Mum, you nearly scared me to death. I thought it was that guy ..."

"I know love, and I'm really sorry. I don't want you to be late for school, that's all."

"S– school?" I frowned up at her. "I ... don't think I can handle school today, Mum. I'm wrecked, nerves all shot. I need a rest. And some Coco Pops in bed."

I shouldn't have added the bit about Coco Pops. I was doing fine till then. Mum laughed and peeled back my duvet. "Come on, young man. There are going to be people all over the flat today. It'll be bad enough, without *you* getting in the way."

I didn't need to be told that. I *knew* there'd be people. That's why I wanted to be there. But it was no good. At ten past eight I was getting into the train as I always did, with my Coco Pops inside me, and my lunch in my bag.

Lee always gets on at the stop after me. I put my bag on the seat as usual, to save it for him. I wouldn't be there to watch the detectives but, hey, I had a seriously good story to tell my mate.

"Hello Alfie," Lee muttered when he got on the bus.

"Hi Lee." I looked at him. "Something the matter?"

"You could say that."

"Why, what's happened?" I asked.

He shook his head. "It's Scott."

"Oh." I knew what he was going to say. It sounds bad, but I'd forgotten all about poor Scott after everything that happened with Smithy. I was just glad I hadn't told the police I'd seen him at the robbery. "In trouble again, is he?"

"Yeah." Lee stared out of the window. "Only went and smashed a jeweller's window, didn't he? In a stolen motor. With two other guys."

"And they were nicked?"

Lee snorted. "*He* was. Scott. The other two scarpered. They left him to drive the car onto waste ground and torch it."

"And did he?"

"Oh yeah. He drove it onto waste ground all right. Just one problem. The place he found

36

was opposite a police station. The second the car went up in flames, the police came running out and arrested him. And now Scott's like, "You don't grass your mates up, it's rule number one." That means he'll go down and his mates can flog all the Rolex watches without him."

I shook my head. "Not this time."

"Huh? What d'you mean?"

So I told him my story, starting with the robbery. "So you see," I smiled when I'd finished, "those two guys are in my photo album with your brother. They'll go down *without* Scott having to grass them up."

Lee nodded. "Well, at least that's something." He frowned. "But who was the guy with the gun? Was he one of Scott's mates too?"

I shrugged. "Dunno. I've been thinking about it. I took some other photos, y'know, up and down the street? Before I saw the robbery. Maybe I got something without knowing it. Something important."

Lee looked at me. "It would have to be something really important, wouldn't it? To make someone want to kill and kill again?"

I had no answer to that. I didn't tell anybody else about what had happened. I don't like people looking at me. Maybe if I said nothing, only Lee would ever know.

Fat chance.

Chapter 8
Like Grass Growing

That day was Friday. It dragged even more than Fridays usually do. I couldn't stop thinking about what was going on at Straw House. What were they doing in my bedroom? What would they be looking for? They didn't need to find the gunman. He was down at the mortuary and going nowhere. What were they looking for then?

And what about my photos? What had happened to them? I'd given my memory card to Detective Sergeant Pitt after Smithy was shot. They'd have examined them by now. Did they show anything? The gunman went to a lot of effort to get the memory card. Was there something that important in the photos? What could it be?

The day didn't half drag on. But, at last, 3:30 snailed by and school packed up for the weekend. Me and Lee got the 3:50 train and sat talking about all those questions till we got to Lee's stop. After that I stared out of the window. 'Can you ever get to sleep in a room where a guy's been shot and killed?' I asked myself.

When I got home I had to use the lift because the first floor landing was still cordoned off.

"Aw come *on*," I groaned as the lift started to go up as slowly as grass growing. 'I'd be faster if I climbed the lift-shaft,' I thought. I hoped my room wasn't still a crime scene, or I'd be sleeping in my parents' room again.

"It's all right, Alfie," Mum said before I had a chance to ask. "They've gone."

"What happened, Mum, did they find anything?"

She shook her head. "Well *I* don't know, do I? They didn't tell me anything. I was only here to let them in and make cups of tea."

"Did they say anything about my photos?"

"I *told* you Alfie, they didn't say anything. Oh, except we can get you a new carpet and claim the money."

"New carpet?"

"Yes, they've taken the old one away because he died on it."

"Glad he didn't die on the *bed*, then. I like my bed!"

Nothing much happened for weeks after that. The police finished on the first floor landing and took the tape away. It was all over the local news, how Smithy got shot in Straw House, and how they couldn't have his funeral because the police were still working on the case. There wasn't anything about me or the guy who'd followed me. Some nosy kids stopped me in the yard and asked me what I'd seen because I lived near the murder scene. I said I didn't know any more than they did, and they left me alone.

Then, just when I thought it had all died down, two police officers came to our flat.

It was a Friday, seven at night. Dad was out. Mum and me were watching telly. Suddenly there was this really loud knock at the door. Mum cracked it open on the chain and there they were. Plain clothes, I.D. cards. Detective Chief Inspectors Lawson and Gill. She let them in and made me turn the TV off. They looked at me and Inspector Lawson said, "Is your name Alfie, young man?"

"Yes sir," I said.

"Well Alfie," he said. "My friend and I have come to thank you."

"*Me?*" I said.

He smiled and said, "Yes Alfie, you."

So Mum sat them down, put the kettle on and this is what he told us.

"We got your photos up on screen straight after you'd given Sergeant Pitt the memory card. We looked hard at them. There were some good shots of the robbery, but we didn't think the shooting was anything to do with that. We thought you must have caught something more serious by mistake. At first we couldn't see anything else important in your photos. They were just photos of a wet street, people walking in the rain and passing traffic. We studied them again, and then we spotted something. Or rather, someone."

Inspector Lawson broke off, smiled and sipped his tea. Inspector Gill took over.

"You'd snapped the entrance to an underground station just as a man was coming out. We thought we'd seen the fellow before, in a photo that the security services had sent out to all police stations. When we had the picture enlarged, all hell broke loose. The man was Vladek Topp. You won't have heard of him, but he's wanted by the police forces of at least 15 countries. He's a terrorist who's known for his attacks on subway systems. He fills them with poisonous gas." Inspector Gill pulled a face. "And you caught him coming out of the underground."

"Oh no," Mum said. "Had he ...?"

"No, no." Inspector Gill shook his head. "He hadn't planted anything. He was probably having a good look round to see where the best place would be. You know, for maximum damage, to hurt the most people ..."

Mum shivered and he went on.

"We got in touch with the security services straight away. The same evening, they carried out raids on a few houses they'd been watching. In one house they found 50 gas canisters hidden in the cellar. Cyanide gas. That's a killer when it's pumped underground."

Then Inspector Lawson started talking again. "The people across the street from the house said they'd seen a man leaving the house that day. He was tall and wore a puffa jacket and a dark baseball cap. Like the man in your photo."

Mum looked at the two officers. "This Vladek character – is he the one that ...?" she began to ask.

Gill nodded. "Yes, he's the fellow who shot Jimmy Smith on your stairs. Later he broke into your home. He'd been careful to make sure he couldn't be identified on any security cameras, but then Alfie took his photograph. It was a complete coincidence, of course, that there was then a robbery. He knew the chances were that you would take your photos to the police. He knew the security services knew his face already and might recognise him. It could be disastrous for him – a wanted killer. He'd have stopped at nothing to get your photo back."

"Yes but …" I said. "How come you guys knew Topp was in our flat?"

Gill shook his head. "We didn't. We asked ourselves why he'd left his safe house. He couldn't have known we were about to raid it. We thought he must have gone after the memory card."

"But he didn't know where I lived."

"We think he must have."

"How?"

"Well, Topp must have found the camera was missing the card a minute or two after you saw him leaving the block after shooting Smith. He *had* to get that memory card. So he came back. When the police arrived to look at Smith, Topp must have hidden somewhere in Straw House. We don't know where he was while you were

45

talking to the police, but he must have somehow managed to follow you and see where you went afterwards. He couldn't do anything with the police everywhere, so he hid and waited. Then he came to your flat later, as you know."

"Ah."

"Anyway, Alfie," said Inspector Lawson, who had finished his tea, "the point is that you probably saved the lives of hundreds of people on the underground. That reminds me ..." He fished in his bag and pulled out my camera. "Is this yours?"

"Hey yeah, looks like it. Where'd you ...?"

Inspector Lawson grinned. "Topp dropped it in a shop doorway and some honest citizen handed it in. Here. I hope it's not broken." He passed it to me, as well as a long buff envelope.

I looked at the envelope. "What's this?"

"It's ... er ... a little something to say thank you from ... well, from some people who think you did very well. Open it when we've gone."

They left soon after that, and then Mum gave me a hug. "Our hero," she said. "Aren't you going to open it?"

I did. Inside was a cheque for £500 and a note that said, 'Sorry about all the fuss with the press.' Mum frowned. "*What* fuss with the press? We haven't *had* any fuss."

Talk about speaking too soon.

Chapter 9
Three Cheers

When Dad came in he had to hear the whole story, then have a drink to celebrate. It was late when I got to bed in the Room of Death, as I called it. I've never *seen* the ghost of Vladek Topp, but it's there all right.

6:30 next morning they arrived. Reporters, photographers. On the walkway outside the flat. Dad had to shove guys aside when he left for work. Mum bolted the door when he'd gone, and even then someone held a mike through the letterbox. "Alfie, a few words for the public, please," he yelled. I went and hid under the bed. On my new carpet. Nightmare.

Mum phoned school and asked if they would excuse me that day. She hadn't let me miss school when it all happened, but I think she found the attention now as scary as I did! The Head said it was ridiculous, holding us prisoner in the flat. He said he'd phone the papers to protest.

If he phoned them, it did no good. The walkway stayed jam-packed. Reporters took turns knocking on the door, and we had to leave the phone off the hook.

By lunchtime Mum had had enough. She called Uncle Harry. He's good in a crisis. He always seems to know what's best to do. He came round, pushed his way through them all and picked a reporter at random. "Want an exclusive?" he asked her. She did, and he hustled her inside. Only then did everyone start to move away.

The reporter was called Pippa. She worked for the *Star* and was nice. She kneeled on my new carpet and asked me some questions. I stayed under the bed. After a bit I came out. By the time she left, the walkway was empty.

You should've seen next day's *Star*. Mum lent Pippa my school photo and there it was, all over the front page. They'd enlarged it about 600 times, and I had a face as big as the town hall clock. 'SNAPSHOT SUPERBOY SCOOPS SPOOK' yelled the headline, in enormous letters.

Then I had to go to school. "Hey!" some idiot shouted, as soon as me and Lee walked into the yard. "It's Snapshot Superboy and his faithful friend."

And if you think *that's* bad, the Head decided it would be really cool to get me up on the platform in assembly and have three cheers. I'm not kidding – three flipping cheers. I nearly died.

It's a bit better now, thank goodness. The robbers are all doing time. They don't know I snapped them, and I'm glad. I didn't want to turn my mate's brother in. There are worse guys in the world than Scott Watford.

But I hope none of them walks into my shot again, that's all.

About the Author

ROBERT SWINDELLS was born in Bradford in Yorkshire. He wasn't clever at school, but he was good at making up stories and he won his first writing competition at the age of 14.

Robert left school at 15 and had lots of different jobs before he decided to train to be a primary school teacher. After several years of teaching, he became a full time writer.

Robert has a Master's Degree in Peace Studies and was sent to jail for seven days for helping blockade Whitehall as a member of the anti-nuclear movement.

Robert has written 70 books for young people and has won the Carnegie Medal, the Children's Book Award (twice), the Angus Book Award, the Other Award, the Sheffield Children's Book Award, and a number of regional prizes.

He lives with his wife on the Yorkshire moors.

*Also by **Robert Swindells** ...*

Burnout

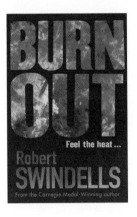

There's one thing I can do really well. REALLY well. I can start fires.

All his life, Josh has felt like a loser. But then he joins Nick Mitchell's gang, and sets fire to his first car. And that blaze lights a spark somewhere in Josh's soul.

But flames spread, and soon Josh's whole life is under threat ...

www.barringtonstoke.co.uk

More from *Barrington Stoke* ...

On the Edge
NIGEL HINTON

Dillon hasn't seen his dad for two years. But now Dad's turned up and he wants to take Dillon and his little brother Robbie on holiday. He says Mum's fine about it.

Robbie's sure Dad has changed but as they set off, Dillon becomes less and less convinced ...

Partners in Crime
NIGEL HINTON

Three best friends.

One hot girl.

Perry's been mates with Todd and Marco for years. They went to school together, now they work in a drugs gang that's made them all rich. But when Perry meets Nadia he sets off a chain of events that can only end in tragedy.

You Killed Me!
KEITH GRAY

Toby is a murderer. That's what the ghost at the end of his bed tells him.

But Toby's just a boy who loves comics, hates cricket, and gets called a geek by his big brother. He'd never kill anyone ...

Or would he?

Johnny Delgado: Private Detective
KEVIN BROOKS

Twenty-four floors up and the only way is down ...

Two gorgeous girls in your bedroom, asking for help. What can you say? Apart from yes.

Private Detective Johnny Delgado has his first case ... but it could also be his last.

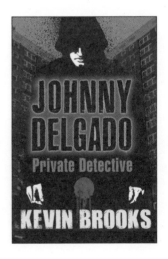

www.barringtonstoke.co.uk